For my mother, my muse — C. H.

Carla Haslbauer was born in Frankfurt am Main, Germany, and grew up in the small town of Bad Nauheim. She works as a freelance illustrator since graduating from the Lucerne School of Art and Design. As a member of the comic collective Corner Collective, she also regularly creates comics. She finds her inspiration in nature and in the everyday life around her. She likes to dig into her childhood memories and finds many stories worth telling. *My Mother's Delightful Deaths* is her first picture book.

Carla Haslbauer

My Mother's Delightful Deaths

Translated by David Henry Wilson

North South

My mother can be lots of different people.

Sometimes she's nice.

And sometimes she's nasty.

Sometimes she's quiet, and sometimes she's loud.

You see, my mother's
an opera singer.

Our new neighbor doesn't know that yet.

My mother plays
many different parts.

Every day she's someone different.

Who are you?

You never know who she's going to be tomorrow.

When she's gone,
we put on our own plays.

We like dressing up as much as she does.

Tonight is the premiere.

My mother loves standing in front of an audience.
What she likes best of all is dying onstage.

She does it differently
every time.

And every time
it looks real.